STONE ARCH BOOKS
a capstone imprint

There Are No Figure Eights in Hockey

by **Chris Kreie**

illustrated by **Jorge Santillan**

Sports Illustrated KIDS

STONE ARCH BOOKS
a capstone imprint

VICTORY SCHOOL SUPERSTARS

Sports Illustrated KIDS *There Are No Figure Eights in Hockey* is published by Stone Arch Books — A Capstone Imprint
1710 Roe Crest Drive
North Mankato, MN 56003
www.capstonepub.com

Art Director and Designer: Bob Lentz
Creative Director: Heather Kindseth
Production Specialist: Michelle Biedscheid

Timeline photo credits: Shutterstock/Chad Willis (top left, flag), Flashon Studio (top left, skates); Sports Illustrated/Bob Martin (bottom left), Heinz Kluetmeier (middle), Richard Meek (top right), Tony Triolo (bottom right).

Library of Congress Cataloging-in-Publication Data is available on the Library of Congress website.
ISBN: 978-1-4342-2071-4 (library binding)
ISBN: 978-1-4342-2808-6 (paperback)
ISBN: 978-1-4342-4977-7 (e-book)

Summary: Champion figure skater Josh challenges himself with the new sport of ice hockey.

Printed in the United States of America in North Mankato, Minnesota.
052015   008920R

TABLE OF CONTENTS

JOSH CHAMPS

AGE: 10   SPORTS: Figure Skating, Hockey
SUPER SPORTS ABILITY: Super skating makes Josh a champion on ice.

VICTORY SCHOOL SUPERSTARS

CARMEN DANNY

KENZIE JOSH

ALICIA TYLER

JOSH

"Man, I love this school," I say to my buddy Tyler. We're walking across the school grounds on the way to practice. I've got my figure skates around my neck, while Tyler dribbles a basketball.

Tyler laughs. "Josh, do you know how weird that makes you sound?" he asks.

"I guess it does. But this isn't a normal school," I say.

"You are right about that," says Tyler.

Here, the sound of sports is always in the air. All the fields, gyms, and equipment are the best money can buy. We are students at the Victory School for Super Athletes. Like all kids at Victory, Tyler and I have super abilities that make us extraordinary at our sports.

"And we are not normal kids," I add. To prove my point, I start spinning with super speed. Even without skates, my feet work like a machine. On the ice, I'm known for my fancy and fast footwork.

"Josh, watch out!" shouts Tyler. I can see that I am going to run into something, but it is just a blur. I try to stop my spin, but it is too late. I run into a bike rack and knock over six bikes.

"Are you okay?" asks Tyler.

"I'm fine. I guess my feet have a mind of their own," I say. "Once they get going, they are hard to stop!"

Tyler and I start standing the bikes back up. "Hey, did I tell you that I am going out for hockey?" I ask.

"No, that's cool. Good luck!" he says.

"Thanks," I say, "but hopefully I won't need luck, not when I have my super skating ability."

I glide backward across the ice. My skates are flying. When I'm on the ice, I feel like I can do anything. I feel like I am completely in charge.

I stop suddenly and push my right skate hard into the ice. Then I jump. In a split second I spin my body around five full times in the air. Then I make a perfect landing back on the ice.

As I land, I hear my best friend, Brendan.

"Nice," he yells, "but remember, there are no figure eights in hockey."

"Very funny," I say.

"I'm just kidding, but you really should get your pads and hockey skates on," he says.

"I know," I say. "I just wanted to warm up first."

"You better hurry," says Brendan. "The rest of the team will be here any minute."

"This is going to be great," I say as I put on my hockey gear. "I cannot wait to play hockey."

"I still don't understand. Why would a figure skater like you want to switch to hockey?" asks Brendan.

"I've already won championships as a figure skater," I say with a shrug. "I want a new challenge."

Brendan nods. "Well, you are going to get it. Get your skates laced up," he says. "Here comes the team."

I turn and look. Then I feel myself gulp. Twelve guys are skating toward us. And every one of them is huge.

I admit it. Hockey is not what I expected. When I first go out on the ice in all my gear, I feel like I can't move. I am used to practicing in lightweight T-shirts and jogging pants. The pads take a little getting used to.

The coach gives us instructions for our first drill. We skate in quick bursts back and forth across the ice. Every time the coach blows his whistle, we stop and skate the other direction. We do it over and over again.

I can't stop like the other skaters. Stopping in hockey skates is totally different from stopping in figure skates. I'm having such a hard time that before I know it, I fly right into the net.

"Hey, new guy," says Colin, one of the other players. "The *puck* is supposed to go into the net, not *you*."

"Thanks for the tip," I mumble.

During the next drill, we all line up and take shots toward the goal. I can't do this either.

Sometimes I don't hit it hard enough, and the puck doesn't even make it half way to the net. The rest of the time, my hockey stick doesn't even connect with the puck.

On my last try, my skates fly out from under me. *Bam!* I fall hard onto the ice. Of course, the other guys laugh again.

"This guy is a joke," says Colin. "Go back to figure skating."

"Don't listen to them," says Brendan. "You're doing fine."

"Yeah, right," I say. I don't feel fine. Thankfully, the next drill is the last of the day.

The coach tells us to skate backward, then switch directions quickly and skate forward to the other end of the rink. This drill doesn't include stopping or hitting. It is a drill of pure speed and footwork. This is what I do. Super skating is my special skill.

I outskate everyone. Each time we do the drill, I'm the first one to the other end of the ice.

"See, you'll be fine," says Brendan at the end of practice. "Meet me back here tomorrow morning. We'll work on a few things."

"I'll be here," I say.

CHAPTER 4

Learning the Basics

Brendan meets me back at the rink the next morning. It is early, so we have the ice to ourselves.

"Let's work on your stopping," says Brendan. "With your super skating skills, you'll learn quickly."

"I hope so," I say.

"Try to skate past me," says Brendan.

"Okay," I say. I skate to one end of the rink and flip a puck onto the end of my stick. Brendan waits for me at the center of the ice.

I dig my skates into the ice and blast forward, right toward Brendan.

When I reach Brendan, I fake to the left, dig my skates hard into the ice, spin around in a full circle, and skate around Brendan to the right.

"Do that again," says Brendan. So I do it again and again and again. Each time I try a new move, and each time I easily skate around Brendan.

"All right, hot shot," says Brendan, laughing. "Now that you can skate, let's work on your shooting."

"Ugh! Don't remind me. My shooting is embarrassing," I say.

"Well, most of us players have been shooting since kindergarten. You didn't learn the basics that we all know," says Brendan.

"Like what?" I ask.

"As you shoot, you have to shift your weight from your back foot to your front foot. All the power will come from your bottom hand," Brendan explains. "Keep that in mind, and try a few wrist shots."

I line the puck up in front of me. As I bring the stick to the puck, I snap my wrist and shift my weight. *Smack!*

The puck lands in the net.

"Hey! It worked!" I say.

"Nice work, but remember that you will have to get past the goalie in a game. The more you practice, the faster that puck will move. And the faster the puck, the harder it is to stop," says Brendan.

"Man, there is so much to learn," I say. "Maybe this was a bad idea . . . me going out for hockey."

"You said you wanted a challenge," Brendan says.

That's true, I did say that.

But I think what I really wanted was to be a star in another sport. I like knowing I am the best at something. But I am definitely not the best at hockey.

"I know. I just think I might be hurting the team," I say.

"You don't have to be perfect, Josh. With your super skating, you have a lot to offer our team. And remember, you don't have to do it all yourself. Learn to work with your teammates," says Brendan.

I think about what he said for a moment. I need to stop thinking about how hard it is and start thinking about how to make my strengths work in hockey. "All right then, teammate," I say, "Let's work on passing."

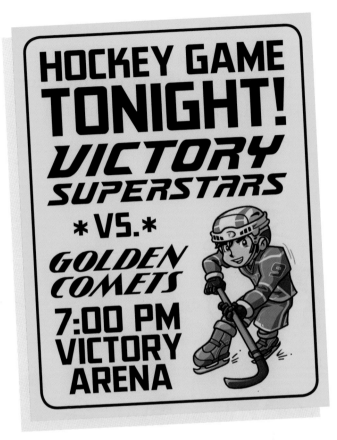

HOCKEY GAME
TONIGHT!
VICTORY
SUPERSTARS
VS.
GOLDEN
COMETS
7:00 PM
VICTORY
ARENA

I've been working hard for a couple weeks now. Today I will see if my work paid off. Today I will try out my skills during a game. The Victory Superstars are playing our biggest rivals, the Golden Comets.

After one period, we are leading 1 to 0. I spent the beginning of the game on the bench. But I'll get my chance to play now, in the second period. I'm nervous. I'm really nervous.

Out on the ice, I can't remember
anything Brendan taught me. I get three
chances to take a shot. But I completely
miss the puck all three times. I let two
Comet players skate right past me for goals.
After two periods, we are losing 2 to 1.

Between periods, I sit by Brendan on the bench.

Colin walks over and stares at Brendan. "Brendan," he says, "didn't you teach the new guy anything? I thought you said you were going to work with him. He still can't play."

"Relax, Colin," says Brendan. "Josh has what it takes. You'll see."

Colin just skates away.

"Josh, what's going on?" asks Brendan. "Where are those moves you showed me?"

"I'm just so nervous out there," I admit.

"Try to relax, okay?" says Brendan. "I'll get you the puck, and we'll show Colin what you've got, all right?"

"All right," I say.

We head back onto the ice to start the
third period. Brendan skates the puck
behind the Comet's goal. "Josh!" he shouts.
"Here you go."

I skate back toward Brendan. He flips
the puck to me. "Now, take it," he says.

I look down the ice. Several Comet defenders are waiting to stop me. I take a deep breath. Then I dig my toes into the ice and take off.

I am a super skater, I tell myself. *I can do this.*

I make a simple
head fake and skate
past the first defender.
I spin around the
second defender
to the left. At the
third defender I stop
quickly, slide the puck
between the defender's
legs, and jump high
into the air to avoid
his stick.

That leaves the goalie. I'd like to shoot and be the guy who ties up the game. But I know my shooting isn't as strong as some of the other guys' — not yet anyway. Colin, our best scorer, is in good position. So I pass the puck his way. Seconds later the puck is in the net, and we've scored.

We all rush over to slap Colin's helmet in celebration. "Nice assist," he says to me.

"What?" I ask.

"That pass. It was an assist. I couldn't have scored without it," he says.

I grin. I just got an assist!

Maybe I'm not a hockey star . . . yet. But I am getting better, and I am part of something I have never been a part of before — a team. And that feels pretty awesome.

"Well, let's do it again," I say. "Let's go, team!"

SUPERSTAR OF THE WEEK
Josh Champs

Josh Champs has long been known for his spins and twirls. So a lot of people were surprised when he started hockey. Since he's put in extra effort to learn the game, he is our Superstar of the Week.

As a figure skater you focus on your own performance. In hockey, you work with a team. How do you like being part of a team?
It is pretty cool. But if you mess up, you let down a bunch of guys. In skating, I only let down myself. But when something good happens out there, we all celebrate!

What would you tell someone who is thinking about trying out for a new sport?
Go for it! But expect to work hard. No one is great without practice, not even if you have a super skill.

What do you like to do when you aren't practicing your sports?
My friends get really annoyed with me because I hardly ever quit practicing. But when I do, we all hang out at the pizza place. At home, I love to watch action flicks.

GLOSSARY

assist (uh-SIST)—when a player helps set up the goal by passing the puck to the goal scorer

celebration (sel-uh-BRAY-shuhn)—a joyous gathering, usually to mark a special event

championships (CHAM-pee-uhn-ships)—contests that determine who will be the overall winner

defenders (di-FEND-ers)—players who try to stop the team with the puck from scoring

embarrassing (em-BA-ruhss-ing)—something that makes you feel awkward or uncomfortable

equipment (i-KWIP-muhnt)—the gear needed to play a certain sport

extraordinary (ek-STROR-duh-ner-ee)—very unusual

footwork (FOOT-wurk)—in skating, clean and steady movement of the feet

goalie (GOH-lee)—someone who guards the goal to keep the other team from scoring

victory (VIK-tuh-ree)—a win in a game or contest

wrist shots (RIST SHOTS)—quick shots made by snapping the wrists forward with the puck against the stick

HOCKEY IN HISTORY

EARLY 1800S — Ice hockey is first played in **Canada**.

1877 — The first known hockey rules are published.

1912 — The number of players allowed on the ice goes from seven to six per team.

1917 — The **National Hockey League (NHL)** is formed.

1946 — Canadian **Gordie Howe** (right) plays his first NHL game. He goes on to play 32 seasons and 1,767 games in the NHL.

1958 — Willie O'Ree becomes the first African-American player in the NHL.

1980 — The **U.S. men's ice hockey team** wins the gold medal in the Winter Olympics. The win is called the "Miracle on Ice."

1994 — Hockey great **Wayne Gretzky** scores goal number 802. He breaks Gordie Howe's record.

1998 — The U.S. women's ice hockey team wins the gold medal in the Winter Olympics. This is the first year women compete in ice hockey.

2010 — **Canada's men's hockey team** wins Olympic gold on home ice.

CHRIS KREIE

Chris Kreie lives in Minnesota with his wife and two children. He works as a school librarian, and writes books like this one in his free time. Some of his other books include *The Curse of Raven Lake* and *Wild Hike*.

JORGE SANTILLAN

Jorge Santillan got his start illustrating in the children's sections of local newspapers. He opened his own illustration studio in 2005. His creative team specializes in books, comics, and children magazines. Jorge lives in Mendoza, Argentina, with his wife, Bety, and their four dogs, Fito, Caro, Angie, and Sammy.